THE CHRISTMAS BLIZZAR

GW00729189

'It's no good,' Daddy said. 'It's freezing hard now. The snow's piled up in a great drift like a tidal wave. We'll never get past it. We're stuck here for the night!'

Sam and her family (not forgetting teddy bear Spud) are going to spend Christmas with Granny and Grandpa. The car is packed with mysterious parcels and Sam is looking forward to all sorts of surprises. But she and her family hadn't expected the adventure caused by a sudden fall of snow.

FAY SAMPSON is the author of 24 books for children, teenagers and adults. Her series of Celtic fantasies about Princess Finnglas and Pangur Bán the white cat is also published by Lion Publishing.

Other Fay Sampson titles
available from Lion Publishing:

Shape-Shifter: the Naming of Pangur Bán
Pangur Bán, the White Cat
Finnglas of the Horses
Finnglas and the Stones of Choosing
The Serpent of Senargad
The White Horse is Running

The Christmas Blizzard

Fay Sampson

Illustrations by Mary Lonsdale

A LION PAPERBACK
Oxford · Batavia · Sydney

Text copyright © 1991 Fay Sampson
Illustrations copyright © 1991 Mary Lonsdale

Published by
Lion Publishing plc
Sandy Lane West, Oxford, England
ISBN 0 7459 2214 7
Albatross Books Pty Ltd
PO Box 320, Sutherland, NSW 2232, Australia
ISBN 0 7324 0527 0

First edition 1991

British Library CIP Data
Sampson, Fay
    The Christmas blizzard.
    I.   Title
    823[J]
    ISBN 0 7459 2214 7

Printed and bound in Great Britain by
Cox and Wyman Ltd, Reading

To Christine

CONTENTS

1
The Box of Surprises

Sam was holding Spud, her teddy bear, in the crook of her arm. Her other hand was playing with the wooden figures in the Christmas crib scene. Her favourite piece, next to the baby Jesus in the manger, was a tiny lamb carried by the smallest shepherd.

Her brother Ian yelled from the top of the stairs, making Sam drop the lamb into the white cotton-wool snow around the stable.

'Isn't Dad home yet? I hope he realizes this lot has got to be packed right at the top. Miss Platt will murder me if they get a hole through the head.'

Mum's voice answered from the hall, 'Your Dad's still not back from work. We can't load anything till he brings the car home. What have you got there, anyway?'

Mum turned to see Ian lurching downstairs with his arms full. Sam giggled. He was carrying a kettledrum, a side drum and a pair of cymbals. Mum's face froze in horror.

'Ian! No drum kit! Absolutely not.'

'But, Mum! It's the jazz concert at school in January. I've got to practise, even if we are going to Granny and Grandad's for Christmas. I've only played *Ma Riley's Black Bottom* once.'

Ian's mother looked him straight in the eye. Even at eleven, he was taller than she was. But Mrs Lawson had the sort of square chin it was a waste of time arguing with, and her gaze was as bright and steady as a policeman's torch.

'Put it this way,' she said: 'there's room in the boot for that drum kit or the Christmas presents, but not both.'

Ian opened his mouth to protest, and then stopped. 'Presents?'

He looked at the mountain of stuff waiting to be packed into the car as soon as Dad got home. The hall was piled high with luggage. You had to climb over it to get to the stairs. There were rolled-up sleeping bags, each one in a different brightly-coloured bag, so that Granny wouldn't need to wash sheets after they had been. There were big blue suitcases for Mum and Dad's clothes, a zipped holdall for each of the children, wellington boots—December in Devon could be very muddy—raincoats.

Sam came padding out of the living-room in her

pink socks.

'You don't take Christmas presents in a *car*.' She said scornfully. 'They come down the chimney, silly. Father Christmas brings them. Everybody knows that.'

'When you're five years old, they do,' Mum said quickly. 'But when you get to my age, let alone Granny and Grandad's, they have to be carried two hundred miles in the back of a clapped-out old Ford in a cardboard box.'

'Talking of clapped-out old cars, where *is* Dad?' said Ian. 'You told me he'd be back before my sausage rolls had finished cooking.'

'Stop fussing. He'll be here soon.'

'Presents in a cardboard box? What cardboard box?' asked Anne, appearing suddenly on the landing. At nine, she was the middle one of the children.

'Nosey,' said Mum. 'Oh, well. I suppose you'll have to see sooner or later. *This* cardboard box.'

She lifted her short legs with difficulty over their heaped-up belongings, stumped up the stairs past Anne, and rummaged in the airing-cupboard. She staggered out again with a huge cardboard box that hid her face.

'Help!' she said, 'I can't see where I'm going.'

'The top step's here,' warned Anne, taking her by the elbow.

Sam stood on tiptoe with excitement as Anne guided Mum down the stairs. The three children bent over to peer into the carton. It was full of parcels wrapped in Christmas paper, holly-green and berry-red. Their eyes lit up as they looked at the shapes. There were all sorts of boxy things, big and small. The thinner, flattish ones might hold books or chocolates. The wider ones could be games, and the chunky ones toys. Then there were mysterious long rolls and exciting lumpy packages.

'Which is for me?' Sam cried eagerly.

'For you?' Mum's eyes were round with surprise, but they were laughing too. 'What a funny idea. I thought you said Father Christmas was delivering yours by reindeer.'

Sam scowled back at her suspiciously. Her blue eyes began to fill with tears.

Anne hugged her sister. 'Don't worry. She's having us on. Those are never all for Granny and Grandad.'

'Well,' Mum admitted. 'There might be the odd one for your father and me, I suppose.'

'And me too! Just a little one?'

Sam's hand stole out and reached for the small cards that said which person each present was for. She twisted one round to look at the writing. She couldn't read very much yet, but she knew that her

own name began with a big curly S for Samantha.

'Ah, ah!' said Mum, smacking her hand away. It wasn't a hard smack; just a joke. 'No cheating! Don't spoil my fun ... Ian, is that your sausage rolls I can smell burning?'

Ian dropped the pair of cymbals he was still carrying with a clang. He vaulted over a heap of sleeping bags, dashed into the kitchen and snatched the oven door open. A thread of blue smoke was rising from one corner of the tray, but the rest of the sausage rolls were a crusty, tempting golden-brown.

'Shame about the burnt one,' he said, flicking it on to the wire tray. 'Can't take that one to Granny's, can I? I shall just have to eat it.'

'Pig,' said Anne. 'Anyway, that means I can try one of your good ones, doesn't it? Ouch! They're hot!'

She gave another one to Sam, who shared the pastry crumbs with Spud. Granny had told them that in Devon they called potatoes 'teddies'. So Sam had christened her teddy bear Spud. He was small and spongy, and his golden coat was already threadbare with so much loving.

'I told you you should have baked those sausage rolls this morning.' Mum had followed them into the kitchen. Her eyes were busy checking the bags of food they had prepared to help out Granny's supplies. 'They won't be cold before Dad comes home to load the car.'

'I wish he'd hurry up,' demanded Anne. 'You said Mr Howard always let them off from the garage early on Christmas Eve. What's keeping him?'

'How should I know? Every other year, they've stopped work for the holiday soon after dinner-time. And he won't have wanted to hang around while the others have a drink, when he knows he's got to drive down to Devon. I was expecting him home before two.'

'It's five to two now,' said Ian.

'Put the radio on, will you?' asked Mum, fidgeting with the cap of a thermos flask. 'We might just catch a weather forecast.'

There was a brief crackle and then: '... The South-West, South Wales and the Midlands: The rain now falling will ease gradually, possibly turning to wintry showers later. These showers will die out overnight. With skies clearing, we can expect a very cold frosty night with icy roads before morning. In the North...'

'Brr!' said Ian.

Mum leaned across him and switched off. 'I could do without his wintry showers, never mind the ice and frost. Come on, Dad!'

'Never mind,' Anne said. 'We'll be tucked up in

15

bed at Granny's by then, won't we?'

'You'll be in bed. I'll be on the floor,' Ian pointed out.

'Spud and I are in bed now,' Sam called from the hall. 'Come and look at us.'

The others went into the hall. Sam had unrolled all the sleeping bags. She was just climbing out of Ian's and into Mum's. She snuggled down until just her nose and Spud's were showing.

'This is the best one,' she said. 'Why can't I have orange roses on mine? It's prettier than plain pink and purple.'

'Sam!' yelled Anne, tugging her hair in despair. She looked at the mess of multicoloured nylon that had been five neat bedrolls. 'You little horror! I spent half the morning rolling those up and squashing them into their bags. I'll kill you.'

Just then, the telephone rang. Anne struggled her way across the muddle and picked up the receiver.

'All right. But I tell you now, she's not going to be pleased.' She held it out. 'It's for you, Mum. It's Dad. It sounds like bad news.'

2
Hurry up, Dad!

Mum listened and sighed. 'All right, then. Just be as quick as you can, love.' She swung round to face them. 'Terrific! They've run into a problem with the car they were working on this morning, and they'd promised the customer he'd have it back in time for Christmas. So your Dad's going to have to stay on till he's got it fixed.'

'But didn't he tell Mr Howard we're going to Devon for Christmas?' protested Ian.

'You know your Dad. A promise is a promise. And he's their best mechanic.'

'Won't we be able to go now?' asked Sam.

'Of course we'll go. We shall just get there later than we wanted to, that's all. I'd better ring Granny and warn her.'

The children drifted back into the living-room. It was a gloomy December afternoon. Anne peered out of the window at the heavy brown sky and the rain dripping off the rose-bushes in the front garden.

'I wish it would snow this year,' she sighed.

'It won't,' Ian said. 'It never does snow at Christmas. That's only on Christmas cards and skiing adverts. All it ever does in real life is rain.'

'I've never seen snow, have I?' said Sam. 'We could make a snowman and have snowball fights.'

Sam was five. Only a week ago Mum had bought her a new yellow raincoat and shiny red wellington boots. Sam had worn them in the rain and stamped in the puddles. But crunching through deep snow in them would be much more fun.

'It seems funny to be going away for Christmas,' said Ian.

He fiddled with the tinsel on the Christmas tree in the window. Even though they were going away, Dad had brought a tree home as usual and put it in a tub. Anne and Mum had decorated it with shiny balls and tinsel garlands. Last of all, Ian himself had hung the lights round it and switched them on. But there were no presents on the tree this year. There wouldn't be any, even though tomorrow was Christmas Day. They were taking all the presents with them to Granny's house. When they came home there would be no left-over turkey and pudding in the fridge, no mess of wrapping paper in the bins. It would be as though Christmas had never happened in this house.

Well, not quite. There was the Christmas crib scene glowing on the shelf in the warm light of the wall-lamp. Sam sat Spud beside it so that he could see better.

'That's Mary, in blue, sitting beside the manger. And that's Joseph beside her. And there are the three shepherds bending over to see the baby. And... *Mum!* Where's the little lamb? I've lost it!'

Panic-stricken, she scrabbled in the soft cotton-wool. At last she uncovered it, a tiny shape of carved wood. She stroked it carefully and set it back in the lamp-lit stable, close to the manger of the baby Jesus.

'There!' she said. 'You'll be safe now.'

'I wish we could go *right* away,' said Anne, still gazing out of the window. But she was not seeing the rainy garden in front of her now. 'Somewhere right up in the mountains. A log cabin, with fir trees all around. And we'd wake up in the morning and hear church bells ringing over the snow. And there'd be footprints of deer and foxes outside the door.'

'And reindeer on the roof!' laughed Sam.

'The sun would be shining on the icicles,' Anne went on dreamily. 'And there'd be a deep, deep blue sky above the mountain peaks.'

'I'm afraid all the Weather Centre can offer you is "wintry showers",' said Ian. 'Tough!'

Outside in the hall, Mum had finished telephoning Grandad and Granny to say they would be late. She was still wandering about restlessly. The hall had looked full before, but she kept adding things to the pile. She brought out the plastic food boxes they used for picnics. Ian lifted the lid of one and peeked inside. There were his sausage rolls.

'What's in the others?'

'I've made us some sandwiches,' Mum explained. 'You never know. I'll fill the thermos flasks just before we go. Mushroom soup and tea.'

'Not in the same flask, I hope,' grinned Ian, and ducked as she tried to hit him. 'What's this all for, anyway? Aren't we going to stop at a motorway service station?'

'Better safe than sorry, especially this time of year. Have you got all your boots and anoraks and gloves and scarves ready? Your Dad will want to be off as soon as he can turn round. There's no need to put everything on. We'll be warm enough in the car.'

'Can't I wear my new boots?' asked Sam.

'If it will make you happy. But don't put them on till it's time to go. And don't forget to bring your slippers. Now ... Anne, first-aid kit and a torch and the book of road maps.'

Mum herself went off through the kitchen. They

heard her opening the back door into the garden and coming in again. This time she was carrying a large shovel.

'You're nuts.' said Ian. 'What's that for? Shovelling coal? Last time I was there, Granny and Grandad's house had central heating and a gas fire.'

'It's not for when we get there,' Mum said. 'It's in case we need it on the way. You never know what may happen in the middle of winter.'

The children looked at each other. The journey was starting to sound like a real adventure, not just one they were pretending.

'You don't think it's *really* going to snow, do you?' asked Anne. 'Not properly? We won't get stuck in it, will we?'

Sam wasn't listening much. Her eyes were still caught by the brightly-coloured packets in the box in the hall. She couldn't help creeping towards it.

'How do I know?' Mum said.' "Wintry showers" they may be. But I like to feel I'm ready for anything, that's all ... Sam! get your thieving little hands out of that box of presents or I'll grind you to powder and stir you into a cup of tea!'

Sam giggled. Ian swung her off her feet and separated her from a large squashy parcel. He looked at the living-room clock. It was just after three. He subtracted that from twelve. 'Only nine hours left till Christmas Day, Sam,' he grinned. 'Can you hold on till then?'

'I hope to goodness you can last a bit longer than that,' said Mum. 'Granny's not going to thank me if you lot are racketing around opening your Christmas presents as soon as midnight strikes.'

'Midnight!' said Anne, hugging herself. 'Midnight at Christmas. We'll be in a strange bed, in a strange house, in a strange part of the country. It'll be a bit like the real Christmas story.'

'Don't be daft,' laughed Ian. 'It's not strange at all. We've been to Granny and Grandad's tons of times.'

'Never in the winter, though,' said Anne. 'They've always come to us for Christmas. This year, it will be quite different. I'm glad it will be dark when we get there. We shan't see anything till we wake up. And then everything will be new. Like a magic land.'

'Granny said Spud and me can sleep in her attic,' said Sam importantly. Then, 'Spud! Mummy, I can't find Spud! Where's he gone?'

She dropped to her knees and crawled frantically under the furniture, calling, 'Spud! Spud! You bad bear. Where are you?'

'Oh, dear, here we go again!' sighed Anne. She walked out into the hall and began to lift coats and holdalls and sleeping bags. There was no golden

teddy bear under any of them. 'Where did you last have him, Sam?'

'I don't *know*, do I?' wept Sam. 'Or he wouldn't be lost. I'm not going without him. I never going anywhere without Spud.'

'Hang on,' said Ian. 'I seem to remember someone playing Goldilocks and the One Bear.' He began to lift the sleeping bags in turn and to feel them. 'This one's too thin . . . and this one's too thick. This one's too hard . . . and this one's too soft. And this one's . . .' He turned Dad's blue-and-black sleeping bag upside-down and shook it. '. . . just right!' Spud tumbled out on to the hall floor. Sam picked him up and hugged him fiercely.

Mum crossed to the window. Already the heavy clouds outside were making it hard to see. The lights on the Christmas tree shone out more brightly in the gloom. The window reflected the glittering balls and the lamp-lit Nativity scene and her anxious face.

'Half past three. Where's that man got to? Arriving at night is one thing. At this rate, it's going to be dark before we even start.'

Ian and Anne caught each other's eyes. This was not going to be like any other Christmas Eve they had ever had, just sitting in front of the television waiting for bedtime. All their friends would be snug indoors. They themselves would be starting out after night had already fallen, to drive two hundred miles in the dark.

It was going to be a bigger adventure than they had realized.

3
Into the Dark

The hands of the clock edged past four in the afternoon. There was still no sign of Dad.

'Come on,' said Mum, jumping up, although she had only sat down two minutes ago. 'We'll have an early tea and wash up, then we shan't need to stop for a big meal on the way.'

'What about Dad?'

'He'll have to grab his while we load the car.'

She got some pies out of the freezer and opened a tin of peas.

'I'm not hungry,' complained Sam. 'It's too soon after that sausage roll.'

'Speak for yourself. It's never too soon for pie and mushy peas,' said Ian. 'Steer yours in this direction if you don't want it.'

'You eat some,' ordered Mum. 'There's no saying when you'll get another meal.'

In a few minutes, the kitchen was looking unnaturally clean and bare again. There was nothing to do but go back to the living-room and slump in the armchairs while they waited. Outside the cars had their headlights on, as they swished along the wet road. The blue-white street-lights had come on too.

Sam felt full and sleepy. She curled up against the cushions and hugged her teddy bear. She wasn't sure if she wanted to go away for Christmas now.

'Can't we sleep in our own beds tonight?'

The others didn't answer her. Suddenly home did seem the best place to be after all. It was very friendly and cosy. Upstairs their warm beds were waiting. Going out into the cold, wet night didn't seem nearly such a pleasant idea now.

Anne had just got up to turn the television on when another set of car headlamps swung round the corner of the road. She recognized the rough note of the engine even before it slowed and stopped outside the house.

'Mum! He's here!' she cried.

Now everything began to happen very fast. Dad came striding up the path, his shoulders looking even broader than usual in his padded ski-jacket. Anne flew to open the door to meet him. He picked her up and kissed her. His face and hands were still streaked with black from the garage where he had been working all day. He smelt of oil.

27

'Gosh, I'm sorry about that, love,' he said, kissing Mum as well over Anne's head. 'Did you think I was never coming? Boss had promised Mr Tapp we'd have his old Cavalier back on the road before we shut for the holiday. We put him new piston-rings in, but when we got it all back together, there was still this tapping noise. Well, we tried all sorts. Boss was afraid it could be the little end going. Wouldn't risk letting it go. Then I had the bright idea that it might just be the timing. And it was. Had it fixed in seconds, after that. Just as well! I could see me still being there at midnight, stripping it down again.'

As he talked, he was already scrubbing his hands at the sink and splashing grey, soapy water everywhere.

'Some Christmas Night that would have been!' scoffed Ian. 'In a garage!'

'The first one was in a stable, wasn't it? Not so different from a garage, if you ask me.'

'Never mind why you're late,' said Mum. 'Just give me the car-keys. There's some pie and peas in the microwave.'

'Did you listen to the weather forecast?'

'Not since two o'clock. Possible wintry showers. Snow over higher ground further north.'

'That's all right. We're heading south. Good job we're going to Devon, not Scotland.'

'Squad fall in,' Mum ordered the children. 'I want that car packed before he's finished eating his tea. Jackets on. No sense in getting cold while you do it.'

Sam struggled proudly up and down the path in her new boots. But it *was* cold, even though they were hurrying backwards and forwards from the front door to the pavement, with their arms full of things. It was not quite freezing, but the sort of damp, nasty cold that gets into your bones and makes your face ache. Sam's arms began to ache too, as she tried to clutch them round her bedroll.

'Watch out! Your sleeping bag's getting all wet,' said Ian, rescuing the folds of pink nylon which were trailing behind Sam down the steps.

'I told you you shouldn't have taken it out of its bag,' Anne scolded.

After that, they let Sam carry the food boxes and the first-aid kit and the torch to the front of the car, while Ian and Anne humped the bigger pieces of luggage to the back.

Mum waited by the boot and packed everything in as it arrived. She had brought the big suitcases first, and put them in the bottom of the boot. The holdalls went on top of that, and she fitted smaller things in the spaces around. Already it was up to the level of the parcel-shelf, and there were still things left.

'The trouble with going away in the winter,' said Mum, 'is that thick clothes take up so much more room.'

'I know!' said Anne. 'Why not put all the sleeping bags in the back seat with us? It would be lovely and cushiony.'

'Hm!' said Mummy. 'I should have thought you'd have been squashed enough already, with three of you on the back seat. Still, it's an idea. I can't get much more than a box of sausage rolls in here.'

'Are you *sure* you haven't got room for three drums?' asked Ian.

'Ian Lawson! I'll use that drumstick over your head if you try that again.'

'You have remembered your presents, haven't you?' Anne asked her.

The ones she herself was giving were safely hidden in her holdall.

'The presents! Help, no! I slipped them into the cupboard under the stairs to keep them out of the way of Sam's fingers.' Mum dashed into the house and came staggering back with the precious cardboard box. 'What a good job you said! It would have been a poor Christmas, wouldn't it, if I'd left all these behind?'

Then of course she had to unpack half the boot and rearrange everything, so that she could get the box in without squashing the carefully-wrapped parcels. At last she slammed the tail-gate shut over it all.

'Right. Now let's pack *you* lot.'

They spread Ian and Anne's sleeping bags on the back seat and the children sat on them, with Sam in the middle. She arranged the other three sleeping bags over their knees and around them. Anne wriggled herself into a cosy nest.

'This is great. It's like being in bed already.'

Sam tucked Spud under the edge of the sleeping bag. There were just his two round ears and his bright brown eyes peeping over.

Mum yelled out to Dad. 'How much longer are you going to take with those mushy peas?'

'Did you put your shovel in, after all that?' Ian teased her.

'Yes, I did, cheeky-face. It's wedged down the side of the boot next to my suitcase. Let's hope we don't need it.'

She sped back indoors. Ian shut the car door and the little light in the roof went out. In spite of the sleeping bags, it seemed dark and chilly.

'I'm keeping my anorak on till the heater gets going,' said Anne.

They saw Mum draw the curtains across the front window. The lights showed dim behind them. Then

31

they went out completely. Now there were only the hall light showing above the door and the coloured pin-points of light from the Christmas tree. Mum and Dad came out and locked the front door behind them.

'You've left the Christmas tree lights on,' Ian called out. 'Honestly, Mum, you'd forget your head if it wasn't screwed on.'

'Wrong, Mastermind. I left them on on purpose, so burglars will think there's someone at home.'

Sam sat up in alarm.

'There won't really be burglars, will there?' she asked, wide-eyed. 'What about all my toys?'

'It's all right,' Anne comforted her. 'They won't know we've gone away, will they? And we've got all our Christmas presents with us.'

'And Spud,' said Sam.

'Shall I drive?' they heard Mum ask. 'Give you a chance to get your breath back.'

'OK. Looks like you're in a hurry to be off.' Dad settled into the passenger seat and grinned over the back at them. 'Though I may have got the worst of the bargain. I don't know which is more trouble, handling old cars or young children.' He put his hands up as Ian brandished a rolled-up comic.

'We'll sort you out,' threatened Ian, 'for keeping us waiting.'

Mum jerked the car into gear, and the journey had begun.

At the end of the road Ian turned for a last look at their house. He could still make out the glowing pyramid of the Christmas tree through the curtains. He had made a good job of hanging those lights. He liked the thought that they would go on shining like that until they came home.

'Just a minute!' said Dad, unsnapping his seat-belt. 'I forgot to phone the AA. I was going to get a last-minute check on the weather and road conditions. Best to be on the safe side, this time of year.'

'Sorry. Can't stop now. We've lost enough time already,' said Mum. 'It's going to be nine o'clock before we get to Granny and Grandad's, as it is.'

They spun round the corner and headed out of town.

As the road climbed they could look down at the city they were leaving. Spread below them were all the strings of lights along the roads, the coloured decorations in the High Street, the illuminated star on the tallest department store. Up ahead of them a circle of golden lights sprang out of the dark, like a giant's necklace. Sam, squashed in the middle, leaned across Anne's knee to see better.

'Look, they've put Christmas decorations up here too!'

'Don't be silly,' laughed Ian. 'This is just the roundabout before you join the motorway. They always have yellow lights over it at night.'

'Then it must always be Christmas,' argued Sam. 'So there!'

The car swept on to the motorway and left the golden necklace behind. It was very dark now. Red tail lights sped in front of them. White and yellow headlights rushed towards them on the opposite carriageway. The windscreen wipers ticked to and fro like the pendulum of a grandfather clock. Sam's head leaned against Anne's arm and her thumb slipped out of her mouth.

For a long time there was not much to see until Mum drove off the motorway and pulled up at a service station.

'Everybody out. Loo stop and a drink. I'll give you ten minutes,' she said.

The car-park was almost empty. It was not at all like the times when they had stopped here on their summer holidays. They seemed to be almost the last people on the road. There was no queue for the toilets or the cafeteria. The children had coke and a mince pie. It was Christmas Eve, after all. But they were not allowed to linger at the table for long.

'All aboard,' said Dad. 'My turn to drive.'

'At least the rain's stopped,' said Mum. 'We

ought to be there in another couple of hours.'

As they stepped out of the warm, lighted cafeteria on to the black car-park, Anne held out her hand to the sky. No raindrops fell on it. But there was a little white speck on the sleeve of her deep-blue anorak.

She stared at it for a moment, feeling a wave of excitement rising up in her. It couldn't really be a snowflake, could it? It was so small. Just one single, tiny crystal of ice. She waited breathlessly for another. It didn't come. She thought of all those magical Christmas scenes on the cards they had left behind them. Were they really going to come true this year? She found she couldn't bear to say anything yet, in case it didn't happen.

'Come on, Anne!'

She brushed the little snow-crystal away and ran to catch up with the others.

4
Stuck!

At the next golden-lit roundabout Dad turned off the motorway. The clouds seemed to have gone. The moon rose, shining down out of a silvery sky to show hump-backed hills and the black lines of hedges. Sam felt her eyes closing again. Beside her, Anne gazed silently at the unearthly scene.

'How's that for Glorious Devon? It feels as though we're getting close now, doesn't it?' Dad called. 'Anybody got room left for one of Granny's suppers?'

'Me!' shouted Ian. 'I'm as hollow as a drum. Sorry, Mum. I didn't mean it!'

'Sh!' said Anne. 'Sam's asleep.'

'I wish you hadn't mentioned supper, Dad,' Ian complained. 'I wasn't thinking about it till then. Can't you go any faster?'

'I could, but I won't,' said Dad. 'A clear frosty night like this, there could be black ice on the road.'

'Why black?' asked Anne.

'Because you don't see it until you hit it. Then the car starts to skate all over the road instead of driving where you tell it to.'

Anne wished she hadn't asked. It sounded scary. Presently they left the wide dual-carriageway for a narrower country road. The way was climbing now, and Dad drove still more slowly. They passed the glow of cottage windows and then there was nothing but the ghostly fields and trees and a black mass of clouds starting to edge up to blot out the stars above the hills.

The moon disappeared as the silver-lined cloud-bank rose higher. Ian waited for it to reappear, but the sky went dark. The fields became as black as the hedges. Ian pressed his face against the window, peering out into the night. At first he thought he could still make out a darker edge where the hills met the sky. Then he lost that too.

'Oh, oh,' said Dad. 'This isn't rain.'

There were white flecks gathering on the wind-screen. He flicked on the wipers and they began to sweep aside a pale crust.

'Is it really snowing?' asked Anne eagerly. 'I caught a snowflake on my anorak when we left the service station.'

'Did you, indeed?' said Dad. 'I wish you'd said!'

'Why?' Anne had been hugging to herself her

dream of a wonderful white Christmas at Granny's house in the country.

'I'd have phoned up while we were stopped and asked the AA what it was like ahead. Found out if it was safe to go on. Oh, well. Let's hope this is just one of Mum's "wintry showers".'

'Don't blame me! I didn't write the weather forecast.'

'Let's see if we can pick up any traffic news on local radio.' Dad fiddled with a knob on the dashboard. 'I always meant to get this thing fixed.'

Mum laughed. 'Typical. You work in a garage, and our car's always falling apart. You know what they say. *Cobblers' children go barefoot, and doctors' wives die young.*'

'Now be fair! This vehicle's safe, even if the radio doesn't work. Anyway, I always seem to be working overtime looking after somebody else's car.'

Ahead, all they could see were two funnels of light, busy with falling snowflakes.

'It looks as though it's only snowing in our headlights,' said Anne.

'I wish it was.'

The car was chugging uphill now. The road surface still looked wet and black, but Ian could see that white was beginning to gather in the long grass at the sides.

'How far do you reckon it is now?' Dad asked Mum.

'Search me. I've lost track of where we are in the dark. But I shouldn't think it can be more than ten miles from where we turned off the main road, can it?'

'We should make it all right, then. After all, this is only Devon. It's not as if we were driving up to Ben Nevis.'

Sam stirred. 'Who's Ben Nevis?' she asked in a small sleepy voice. 'You said we were going to Granny's for Christmas.'

'Hullo! I thought you were getting some shut-eye.'

'Not who. What,' Ian told her. 'Ben Nevis is in Scotland. It's the highest mountain in Britain.'

'Don't worry, love,' Mum laughed. 'We're not going anywhere near Scotland. At least, I hope not!'

'If you keep on going past Granny's, you come to Dartmoor,' said Ian. 'It snows there, all right.'

'What do you think?' Dad asked Mum. 'Next house we come to, we could stop and phone your mother. Ask what it's like out her way and warn them we may be held up if it comes down thick.'

'Chance would be a fine thing,' Mum said. 'Do you see any sign of human habitation?'

'Keep your eyes skinned, everybody,' Dad

ordered. 'Sing out if you see a light.'

The white snowflakes were falling on to a white road now. The windscreen wipers swept smaller and smaller arcs as the snow piled up against the glass.

Sam stared at it in fascination. 'Look, Spud,' she whispered. 'That's real snow.'

Spud seemed to be whispering something back into her ear. 'He says he didn't think there would be such a lot of it.'

'Nor did I,' said Dad grimly. 'And I don't like the way the wind is getting up. Look at it driving the flakes sideways.'

'There!' called Ian, after a while. 'I think that's a house down below the road.'

'Where?'

'You've passed it now. It was back there on the left.'

'Very far off the road?'

'I couldn't see properly. It was just a sort of dim glow.'

Dad sounded doubtful. 'I'm not sure I could turn the car round in the lane just here, even if I wanted to. And I'd rather not stop on this hill if I can help it. Try and give me a bit more warning when you see the next one.'

But there wasn't a next one. It was like driving into a speckled fog. It was hard even to see where the sides of the road were. Anne thought of the tiny crystal of ice lying on her anorak sleeve. That was all this was. Millions and millions of those crystals tumbling out of the sky all around them.

The road was getting steeper and more slippery. For a long time nobody spoke. Dad wrestled with the steering-wheel, while the others stared anxiously out of the window.

There was a bend in the lane ahead. As the wheel turned, the car jerked and slithered. Dad changed gear and revved up. They lurched forward a little way and stopped again. The engine roared and strained, but this time they did not move.

'Sorry, folks. That's it. We're stuck. She won't get up this hill.'

For a moment no one moved while they tried to take in what he had said.

'Aren't we going to get to Granny and Grandad's?' Sam asked. Nobody answered.

Then Mum flicked her seat-belt undone. 'OK. Now do you think I'm nuts, Ian? Aren't you glad I packed a shovel?'

'Good girl!' said Dad. 'I remembered to check the tyres and put in antifreeze, but I never thought of that.'

The two of them put on their coats and got out of the car. As they opened the tailgate a violent, cold wind blew down the children's necks, making them cry out in protest. They heard the scrape of the shovel on the hard road. Dad was digging the snow away from the wheels, while Mum held the torch. Soon the two grown-ups were shaking the snow off themselves and climbing back into the warm car.

Sam giggled. 'You've got snow on your eyebrows.'

Dad twitched them at her.

'It's my Father Christmas impersonation. Sit tight. There's a devil of a wind behind this snow, but I don't think it's too deep yet. If we can just get to the top of this hill we might make it the rest of the way. Good job I've got a good tread on the tyres.'

The children held their breath. This time the car moved forward. But a few metres further the wheels started to slip again.

Mum grasped the shovel and started to open the door.

'Hang on,' said Dad. 'We can't keep digging ourselves out every few minutes. I'm going to see what it's like up ahead.'

'Torch,' said Mum, handing it over. 'And don't go too far. We don't want you getting yourself lost.'

'There's only one road as far as I can see. But keep the engine running and the headlights on, so I can see where you are.'

He set off up the hill in front of them, with his shoulders bent and the hood of his ski-jacket pulled over his head. Long before he should have been out of reach of the headlights the whirling snowflakes had hidden him from them.

'He won't really get lost, will he?' asked Sam. The pelting blizzard looked very different from the cottonwool around the carved stable at home. The little lamb had been hard to find, even in that.

'Not unless he jumps over a hedge and bank three metres high. Don't worry,' Mum reassured her. 'He can see our lights, even if we can't see him.'

All the same, everyone was staring silently into the blizzard watching for him to appear again.

When he struggled back into the light at last, even Sam didn't laugh at him. Snow had plastered itself to his chest in a white blanket. His nose and lips were purple with cold. Mum reached for the thermos flask and poured him some mushroom soup.

'It's no good,' he said, shivering as he took the hot cup from her. 'It's freezing hard now. I had a job to stay on my feet. And when you get to the top of the hill the wind's full in your face. Cuts straight through you, like a skewer through a sausage. It's piling the snow up in a great drift like a tidal wave, as fast as it falls. We'll never get past that.'

'What are we going to do, then?' asked Ian. 'Slide

backwards like a toboggan to the bottom of the hill?'

'Don't talk daft. I'm afraid we've no choice. We're stuck here for the night!'

5

Midnight on the Hill

'But we can't stop here!' said Mum.

'What am I supposed to do? Magic a snow-plough out of thin air?' Dad shouted.

'But Granny and Grandad are expecting us. When you were late, I rang to tell them we'd probably arrive around nine. They'll be worried stiff if we don't show up.'

'I can't help that, can I? It's your fault. You were rushing me to get off, before I'd hardly had a chance to sit down. And then you wouldn't let me go back and phone for a weather report.'

'You could have done it when we were at that service station. If we'd set off at two like we planned, we'd have been there by now.'

It was scaring for the children, listening to the two grown-ups arguing. It made it seem as though nobody knew what to do. Dad got control of himself first.

'Sorry, love. Look. We're in a fix. No good

blaming each other, is it? We've got to think what's the best thing to do now.'

'Couldn't we keep digging our way out bit by bit, till the road gets better?' Ian suggested.

'You haven't been out there. It's coming down faster than we could clear it. A proper blizzard. And it's even worse when you get over the top.'

Dad pressed a switch and the headlamps went out. He turned off the engine. At once, the wild, whirling whiteness became dark night, pressing up against the windows. Even the lights on the dashboard had gone out. The car creaked and groaned as the metal began to cool. In the darkness Anne felt Sam cuddle closer against her.

'We'll just have to walk to the next house and ask if we can use their phone. Surely the people there would let us sleep on their floor,' Mum said. 'We can't stay here and freeze to death.'

'That last house Ian saw was a mile or two back. I couldn't see a sign of anything up ahead. I could hardly see my nose in front of my face, the snow's coming down that thick.'

'But there must be houses, mustn't there? A farm, or something. It's funny how you don't notice when you're whizzing along the road in the summer.'

'How far? Fifty yards? A couple of miles? That snowdrift at the top of the hill was as high as my head already. We can't just march off into a blizzard with no idea where we're going.'

'You should always stay with the car,' Ian said. 'The police said that on *Blue Peter*. So they know where to find you when they send the rescue helicopter out.'

'A helicopter?' Sam marvelled. 'For me and Spud?'

'Is that really what they'll do?' Anne asked. 'Fly over and lift us off? I'd be scared stiff, swinging around up there over the tops of the trees. But won't it be brilliant afterwards, when we tell everybody at school?'

'Well, you're in for a long wait. They're not going to find us in the dark in the middle of a snowstorm, are they?' Ian scoffed.

'More likely a council snow-plough in the morning,' Dad said. 'Hey! Do you suppose they work Christmas Day?'

'Terrific!' Mum sighed. 'I'd almost forgotten it was Christmas Eve. This is going to be a very peculiar Christmas, folks.'

'Never mind,' Anne comforted her. 'What a good job you made us bring our sleeping bags and pack all that food.'

'It was only a few last-minute sandwiches. The rest was meant to save Granny spending half her holiday in the kitchen. Overnight camping supplies

49

were definitely not part of the plan.'

'They ought to sack that weather-man. Wintry showers!' said Ian. 'Some shower, this is. I wouldn't like to try what they call a *real* blizzard.'

'We can all make mistakes,' said Dad. 'I should have checked up when we stopped for petrol. We could have stayed at that service station. At least we'd have been in the warm and had plenty of hot food.'

'Switch on the engine again, Dad,' said Anne. 'I'm getting cold.'

'Sorry. No can do. Not unless you want us to be poisoned. You get carbon monoxide fumes if the car's standing still and the snow builds up over the exhaust pipe.'

'You mean we've got to freeze all night?'

'Not if I have anything to do with it,' Mum said. 'I knew there must be a reason for bringing all those clothes. Ian, can you lift the parcel-shelf off and winkle some jumpers out of the cases?'

She switched on the little light in the roof. Ian knelt on the seat and half disappeared over the back. There was a lot of pulling and pushing and grunting as he wrestled with the cases squashed in the boot.

'Mind the Christmas presents!' ordered Sam fiercely. 'I'll set Spud on you if you break any.'

'Mind me!' Anne protested. 'That's only my

thumb you're kneeling on.'

Soon everyone was padded out with extra sweaters and their thick jackets over the top. They even put their woolly hats and scarves and gloves on to keep ears and fingers warm.

'Right,' said Mum. 'I don't suppose anyone's going to laugh at my hot soup now.'

'Oh, no!' Ian said fervently. 'I think you're brilliant.'

'I don't know so much about that. Your Dad's right. I got in a rush, because I didn't want Granny and Grandad to be worried. Now look where it's landed us.'

They had to take off their gloves again. The hot cups warmed their fingers while they drank cups of mushroom soup and ate corned beef sandwiches and some of Ian's sausage rolls and the chocolate log Mum had meant for Christmas tea. Sam looked up at all the bigger people squashed around her.

'It's like being in a cave, isn't it? Spud says bears always spend Christmas like this. Teddy bears like picnics.'

'I'm glad somebody's pleased,' said Dad. 'I'm not.'

'I don't suppose I could have a cup of tea as well, could I?' Ian pleaded, looking mournfully at his empty cup. 'My sausage rolls were fantastic, of course, but they weren't hot.'

'Tough,' said Mum. 'I'm saving the rest for breakfast. Lukewarm tea's better than nothing. It's not quite the same as bacon and egg, but it's the best I can manage under the circumstances. Right! If anyone wants the bathroom, you'll have to hop out into the snow. And be quick about it. Then you'd better get right inside your sleeping bags.'

'Just a minute,' said Dad. 'Pass those holdalls over, Ian.'

He wedged the bags between the seats to make a wide flat bed. Before long they were all tucked up to their ears and curled up wherever they could find room for their bent legs. Dad switched out the light, then leaned across Mum. The handle of the window creaked.

'Hey! Where's that draught coming from?' cried Ian. 'It's like an ice-edged razor-blade!'

'Sorry, old son. But it's either that or we all stop breathing. There's hardly enough air in this car to last one person the night, never mind five. I opened your side because the snow's blowing on mine.'

'We won't really freeze to death, will we?' asked Anne.

Mum reached out between the seats and squeezed her hand. 'Not likely! Wrapped up like sausage rolls and with all that hot soup inside us?'

'Not unless you stick your bony knees any

further into my back and I throw you out into the snow,' Ian complained. 'Can't you lie any straighter?'

'No,' said Anne. 'This car isn't big enough. Sam's lying across my legs, as it is.'

'Be quiet, everybody,' said Sam. 'Spud and me are trying to get to sleep. It's Christmas Eve. Father Christmas won't come if you keep on talking.'

There was silence for a while. Then Anne started to giggle.

'Won't it be silly if we wake up in the morning and find we're parked outside somebody's front gate?'

'That happened to us once, before you were born,' Dad chuckled. 'Mum and I were driving round Ireland on holiday and we got lost in the fog. We saw what we thought was a patch of grass and put the tent up for the night. Next morning I crawled out in my pyjamas and found we'd camped on this traffic island on the outskirts of Dublin. All the locals were driving round us on their way to work, grinning like mad!'

A few moments later Anne heard him snoring gently, and then they were all asleep.

When Anne woke, she was cold and cramped. It was still pitch dark. Carefully she wriggled up into a sitting position. Ian groaned and tried to turn over in his sleep. Anne rubbed the window. Snow was piled up in the corners, but through the cold glass she could just make out the glimmer of snowy fields under a black sky. Mum stirred on the seat in front of her.

'What's your problem? Are you all right?'

'I'm just a bit stiff, and my left leg's got pins and needles,' said Anne. 'I think it's stopped snowing.'

'Thank heavens for that. At least we shan't be completely buried under a snowdrift.'

'What time is it?'

Mum fumbled under layers of sleeves to find her watch.

'One minute to twelve.'

Anne caught her breath. She counted sixty slowly. Then she smiled in the darkness.

'Midnight! Midnight on Christmas morning! I'll never forget this Christmas; will you? It's a bit like Joseph and Mary and Jesus, not being able to find a bed in Bethelehem, isn't it?'

'I must say the thought hadn't occurred to me. But now you come to mention it, I suppose that's one way of looking at it. I hope it wasn't as cold a night as this for the baby Jesus.'

'Happy Christmas!' whispered Anne.

'Happy Christmas, love,' Mum whispered back.

Then they both cuddled down to try to sleep again on that strangest Christmas night.

Presently Anne murmured, 'Mum? Can you hear something?'

'It's all right. It's only your Dad snoring.'

'No! Nicer than that,' Anne giggled. 'High and far away.'

Mum listened. 'I can hear the wind whistling through that slit at the top of the window. Was it that sort of something?'

'I don't think so. I believe I can hear bells. Like a church. Can't you?'

'Bells? Out here?'

'Ssh! Don't talk about it. Just listen.'

After a little while Anne asked again, 'Mum, how long do you think it will be before somebody finds us?'

This time there was no answer.

6

The Expedition

Everybody woke early that morning. A weird, white light filled the car. Ian rubbed at the window.

'Funny,' he said. 'I can't see out.'

'We're snowed in!' exclaimed Anne.

Snow was packed against the windows on three sides. On the fourth, the glass was crazed with frost, inside as well as out. It was bitterly cold.

The others struggled to sit up, shivering as their heads and shoulders left the warmth of the sleeping bags.

'Happy Christmas, everyone,' said Mum, for the second time that day. 'In case you'd forgotten.'

'Mummy!' cried Sam in horror. 'I forgot to hang up my stocking!'

The other four burst out laughing.

'Well, if that was the only thing that went wrong last night, we shouldn't have much to worry about,' said Dad.

'It's OK, Sam,' Mum reassured her. 'You don't

think Father Christmas would be put off by a little bit of snow, do you? If you look in the boot, I think you'll find the reindeer got here.'

'My boot!' Sam dived under the seat to find her red wellingtons. She shook them both upside-down. 'They're empty!' she wailed.

'Not that boot, pin-head,' Ian grinned. 'She means the car boot.'

The three children peered over the back seat, and there, under the shelf, was the mysterious box of Christmas parcels, all wrapped up in green and red paper with patterns of holly and robins. Sam's face lit up like sunshine.

'You cheat! You said they were for Granny and Grandad. They *were* for us!'

'Well, some of them. All right, then, most of them. You can look at the labels now.'

'Oh, come on, love!' Dad groaned. 'You're not going to let them start opening them here, are you? There's hardly room to move without getting an elbow in your eye.'

'Just one!' begged Sam. 'One each?'

'Hang on a bit,' Dad said. 'I want to take a reccy first. Get some idea where we are.'

He pushed at his door. Nothing happened.

'Can you get yours open?' he asked Mum.

She heaved against the side. The door gave a

centimetre or two, and then stuck. The two of them looked at each other.

'Anne was right. We *are* snowed in,' Mum said. 'Now what do we do?'

'There's the window,' said Ian. 'I can just see out of the top of it on Mum's side, so we can't be buried right up to the roof.'

Every time anyone spoke their breath came out in puffs of vapour. But through the steamy air they could peer through the open slit above Mum's head. Beyond the roadside they had a glimpse of chilly white fields under a grey sky. The hedge had almost disappeared under a mound of snow that bent its branches. There was no sign of the sun.

'OK. Let's give it a try.'

Mum wound at the window handle and forced the glass down past the clinging wall of snow. She reached out and scooped more snow away. Even on this sheltered side of the car it was over knee-deep. More cold air came blowing through the open window. A load of snow slid from a nearby tree and flopped into the drifts below. The wind blew loose snow across the field like smoke.

'This is like an igloo, isn't it?' said Sam. 'We've got our very own snow-house. Hurry up. I want to open my presents.'

'The faster we get out of this, and into a real

house, the better I shall be pleased,' said Dad. 'But I can't see me getting through that window, padded up like this. What I need is a couple of small, fit volunteers to climb out and dig the snow away from the door, so that larger persons can then make a dignified exit.'

'Me!' 'Me!' cried Anne and Ian.

'Me and Spud!' shouted Sam.

'I said small, not midgets,' Dad smiled at Sam. 'If I drop you two to the bottom of that snowdrift, it would be over your heads. We might never see Spud again.'

Sam clutched her teddy to her. 'Spud didn't bring his wellies. He says he'd rather wait in the car, after all.'

Ian went first. It was a tight squeeze. He was growing fast for eleven, all arms and legs. The snow had a thin, icy crust. There was nothing to hold on to. His top end could only flounder, face down in the snow, while he wriggled his hips and Mum pushed at his legs. At last he made it, though the snow got inside his clothes in all sorts of uncomfortable places. Anne came next. She was smaller and it was easier for her, because she had Ian to pull her as well as Mum to push.

Dad climbed over the driver's seat to the back of the car. After a lot of bother he managed to pull out the shovel again and pass it to them. The two children took turns digging the snow away from the side of the car.

'Here. Have a go with this,' said Mum, passing an empty picnic box to Anne.

The snow flew faster, as Anne scooped while Ian shovelled till his arms ached.

'Phew,' he gasped. 'Want to change over? It's harder work than it looks.'

They were both panting when at last the red metal of the car door stood free.

'My face is hot, but my feet are *freezing!*' Anne complained.

'What, no red carpet?' Mum said as she stepped out to join them.

Next came Dad, who immediately seized the shovel and did some more digging himself. Sam had pulled on her red boots. She followed very carefully, leaving Spud on the back seat.

'You stay there,' she warned, 'until I'm quite sure it's safe for you.'

'Well,' said Mum, crossing her arms and shivering. 'There's not a lot to see, is there?'

There wasn't. Only the snowy humps of the hedge-tops showed where the road was. The banks went on up the hill and back down the way they had come. Fields sloped above them on either side of the road. There was no sign of a house.

'We'll need to get to the top of the hill and have a look-see,' said Dad.

'Oh, no. Not without breakfast,' Mum said. 'Such as it is.'

'The presents! The presents! You said we could open them,' begged Sam.

'Can't I have breakfast first?' groaned Ian. 'I'm famished, after all that shovelling.'

'Go on with you,' Mum laughed, pushing him towards the car. 'It's Christmas Day, isn't it, even if it isn't quite the way we planned it. We shan't get any peace till Sam's got that wrapping paper off. If you're very good, you might even find there are one or two parcels for you.'

Anne sighed patiently, 'It's no good, Ian. You ought to know what Mum's like. What she really means is that she can't wait to open her own presents!'

'Have I got any?' Mum looked surprised.

'Yes,' said Anne. She climbed on to the back seat, rummaged in her holdall and handed over a prettily-wrapped packet. 'Merry Christmas again.'

Sam pushed her way under Anne's arm. 'Mine! Mine!' She gave Mum a little flat present wrapped in blue foil, but she couldn't wait for Mum to open it.

'It's a diary. I've stuck stars in it for all our

birthdays, so you won't forget. Dad helped me a bit.'

'Me?' said Mum. 'Forget your birthday?'

They all piled back into the car after Anne. A lot of snow came with them.

'Very clever,' said Mum. 'Sam was right. We should have had the presents and breakfast first before we got out. When this lot starts to melt, we shall be swimming in it.'

Soon there was a cheerful chaos in the car. It was full of the crackling of paper, shouts of surprise and delight, thank-you hugs and kisses. Then it was time to tidy up, so that nothing would get lost or broken. All the toys and books, and Dad's new jumper and Mum's computer game, were put back as neatly as they could manage into the boot. The torn wrappings were gathered up. They were damp and soggy now from the melted snow on the floor.

'*Now* can I have breakfast? I could kill for a sausage roll,' Ian threatened.

Mum rummaged in the picnic bag. The tea in the flask was almost cold, and there were not many sandwiches left. They munched the rest of the sausage rolls hungrily.

The food was soon finished. The excitement of opening the presents had faded. All the Christmas things had been packed away. The car began to seem cold and still and lonely again.

'I wish it would thaw,' Anne said. 'Then perhaps my fingers would too. They're so cold, they hurt.'

'Not much of a Christmas breakfast, was it?' Ian asked wistfully. 'No bacon and mushrooms.'

'Here,' said Mum. 'Would this cheer you up?'

She opened a huge box of chocolates Dad had given her and passed them round.

'Is that it, then?' said Dad, licking his fingers. 'Let's hope we get out of here by lunchtime. I'd rather have a leg of turkey than a coffee cream, any day. Does anyone feel like an expedition to the Pole?... No? You disappoint me. I was only thinking of that telegraph pole at the top of the hill.'

'I'll come!' said Anne.

'Shouldn't we stay with the car?' Ian reminded him.

'Somebody should. I'm not planning to go out of sight of it. But we'd look pretty silly sitting here in the cold if there's a house just over the hill.'

'Sam and Spud and I will look after the car,' volunteered Mum. 'Won't we Sam?'

Sam looked doubtful. The snow had got inside her red wellington boots and her socks were cold and wet. But she didn't want to be left behind.

'I could leave Spud with you.'

'I'm not sure he'd like that. And you wouldn't want to leave all the presents here by themselves, would you?'

'Tell you what, Sam,' said Dad. 'Could I borrow that red shirt you've got in your case?'

'Why? You're too big to wear it,' Sam giggled.

'It's not for me. It's for the car.'

He scooped around in the deep snow on the car bonnet till he found the radio aerial. He pulled it up as high as it would go.

'Good job we've still got the old-fashioned sort.'

He broke a tall thin branch from the hedge and strapped it to the aerial to hold it upright. Then he tied the sleeve of Sam's shirt to the highest twig. It flapped above the roof of the car like a red flag.

'There! Now nobody will mistake you for a snowdrift. I should hate to see a snow-plough come along and scoop you up.'

'Nobody's going to scoop up Spud,' said Sam fiercely. 'I wouldn't let them!'

'You see that they don't. I'm putting you in charge.'

Dad started off up the road. As soon as he left the trampled snow around the car, he plunged up to his chest. Ahead, the drifts between the banks rose almost to the tops of the hedges.

'It's no good that way,' he said, struggling back. 'The snow's been trapped by these high banks and it's filled the whole lane. It will be over our heads before we get to the top of the hill. We'll have to try

the fields. The wind may have kept the snow moving a bit more in the open.'

Ian and Anne ploughed after him to the nearest gate and climbed over. They jumped into soft snow on the other side. It came up to Dad's thighs. But it was not too deep for him to struggle through it, flattening a track for the older children to follow.

He called back to Mum and Sam.

'If we do see anything hopeful from the top, we'll signal to let you know which way we're going.'

The members of the expedition waved. Then they began to clamber away from the car up the white field. Three figures in coloured jackets, one tall, two shorter, getting smaller and smaller in the distance.

Behind them, Sam's red shirt flapped limply under a sunless sky.

Sam crawled over to the front seat and snuggled against Mum.

'Spud and I thought you might be feeling lonely.'

'I was a bit,' said Mum.

7
Rescue

It was hard work, walking in the deep snow. Dad
went first to force a path. He lifted each long leg as
high as he could and pushed it through the snow. Ian
came next, trampling it down underfoot. Then Anne.
But even she sank in nearly up to her knees, which
made her lurch from side to side at each step. She was
glad she had brought her wellingtons, even if they
weren't bright red ones like Sam's. Snow caught on
the tops of her boots and fell coldly inside.

'This is like Good King Wenceslas,' Ian shouted
back to her. '*Mark my footsteps, good my page.*'

They all started to sing.

> 'Good King Wenceslas looked out,
> On the feast of Stephen,
> When the snow lay round about,
> Deep and crisp and even.'

It was even harder, singing as well as ploughing
through the snow. Their breath came in steaming

gasps. But it made them feel more cheerful.

When they got to the last verse,

> 'Heat was in the very sod,
> Which the saint had printed,

the melting snow-water had just reached Anne's toes.

'Judging by the amount of heat in *this* sod, your saintliness rating must be about D-minus, Dad!' she complained.

'Cold feet, warm heart, that's me,' Dad yelled back.

'Anyway, it's not the feast of Stephen till tomorrow,' called Anne. 'How about:

> 'In the bleak midwinter
> Frosty wind made moan.
> Earth stood hard as iron,
> Water like a stone.'

By the time they had finished that carol, their legs were aching with having to be pulled out of the snow and lifted up so high. And their throats were rasping with the cold air. But Dad's deep voice led them rousingly in:

> 'God rest you merry, gentlemen,
> Let nothing you dismay.

Remember Christ our Saviour
Was born on Christmas Day.'

That kept them swinging up the last steep slope to the top of the hill.

All this time the sky had been grey and the snow a joyless, cold blue-white. From time to time a sneaky wind shook the piled snow from the black twigs. As they reached the hilltop, the sky all round them began to flame with red. Even the misty air under the trees started to glow, as if with firelight. The very snow seemed stained with colour. Just as they came over the crest, the sun rose behind them in a huge, scarlet ball. The new landscape at their feet sprang out in dazzling light. It was so bright they could hardly bear to look at it.

There was another valley, with a farmhouse close below them. Smoke was rising from its chimney. Not far beyond lay the little grey town, where Granny and Grandad had moved to live when they retired. Its roofs glittered in the sun. And massed above it, on the skyline, were the huge, humped tors of Dartmoor. They stood blindingly white in the sunlight of Christmas Day.

In that magical moment of brilliant sunrise over a frozen world, even the sight of a house so near seemed unimportant. For a little while, no one spoke.

Then Anne squeezed Dad's hand.

'It's like . . . as if the world has been made new, all over again, because Jesus has come. I wish Mum and Sam could see this.'

'Hold on! Perhaps they will. I think the rescue service is on its way. Look!'

A tractor was starting to climb the field from the farm, leaving dark furrows across the sparkling sheet of snow. It was a distant, deep-blue messenger of hope, like an approaching lifeboat. The three of them shouted and waved to it.

'What's that?' asked Ian suddenly. 'Something moved over there in the hedge.'

'I can't see anything,' Dad said. 'I expect the sunshine's playing tricks with your eyes. Or else the snow is beginning to melt and you saw it dropping off the branches.'

'No. There it is again, Dad! There's something *under* the snow.'

This time they all saw it. The snowdrift was stirring, as if with a very small earthquake.

They ran towards it, or tried to, because it wasn't really possible to run in this deep, fresh snow. Ian fell on his face, but floundered on as fast as he could. His brown-gloved hands scrabbled away at the drift, throwing the snow aside like a rabbit burrowing. Anne came to help him, and then Dad with his big hands in their driving gloves.

At last they began to see something, a patch of sodden, yellowish wool.

'It's a sheep!' cried Ian. 'It must have got buried in the snowdrift.'

'Which end is its head?' panted Anne.

They raced to free her. As they scrabbled the last of the drift away, a broad, curly back emerged. Then there was a puff of snow and a jet of vapour as her head broke free and she gasped for air.

'Look. She's made a snowhouse,' said Anne. 'Like Sam suggested.'

Under the thorny branches of the hedge, the sheep had taken shelter. As the blizzard deepened she had hollowed out a little cave for herself against the bank.

'What a good job you spotted her. I don't know how much longer she could have lasted without fresh air,' Dad said.

The sheep was struggling to her feet, free now of the weight of snow piled over her. She stood unsteadily, heaving and giving little moaning bleats.

'Is she all right?' Ian asked. 'She doesn't look very well.'

'Hurry!' Anne yelled, beckoning to the tractor. It seemed to have stopped between them and the farm. Then, 'Hey! I don't think it was us they were coming out for, at all! There are lots more sheep. It's them they've come to rescue.'

'First things first,' said Dad. 'We're in better shape than this ewe.'

There were two men with the tractor, one very small and one very large. They were halfway up the field now. They kept stopping the tractor and getting down to probe the drifts under the hedge with sticks. They seemed to know just where to look. Time and again they dug in the snow and pulled out a fat, struggling sheep, which they lifted into the box-trailer behind the tractor.

Anne turned back to their own sheep. There were drops of blood in the snow beneath her.

'Dad!' she cried. 'She *is* ill!'

The ewe panted and heaved. Something dark and glistening was starting to fall from under her.

'Is she going to die?'

The men with the tractor had spotted them and it came chugging up the hill. Four huge wheels, with deep-cut tyres, strained to get a grip in the snow. The engine roared in low gear. The rescued sheep huddled in the trailer behind. The smaller man ran ahead of it. He was older than Dad, short and sturdy, with round red cheeks and bright blue eyes. The blue tractor heaved itself over the last fold of the hill and stopped near them. The other man swung himself down from the driving-seat and strode across the snow more slowly. He might have been the first man's son, a fat giant of a young man with curly brown hair. He seemed to the children to be four times the size of the older farmer, but with the same rosy cheeks and merry eyes.

'We dug her out of the snow,' Ian called to them, pointing to their sheep. 'But there's something wrong with her. Can you help her?'

The small man gave a cheerful cackle of laughter.

'Nothing wrong there, boy. You've got her out just in time, by the look of it.'

'But what is she doing?' The blood and the black shiny thing hanging under the ewe frightened Anne.

The little man put his hand on Anne's shoulder. It was warm and steady.

'Don't you worry, my handsome. Just you watch now. She's got something to show you there, better than any Christmas present you've ever had.'

A round black lump, two thin black things, like dangling sticks. There was still more being squeezed out. Then, in a rush, it all slid to the ground, with a little pool of steaming liquid. The ewe turned and began to lick it busily.

'Whatever is it? Is she eating it?' Ian asked.

The black bundle on the ground squirmed, knelt, and staggered upright on four spindly legs.

'It's a lamb!' cried Ian and Anne and Dad all at the same time.

The other two men burst out laughing and clapped each other on the back. Already the tiny lamb was tottering to its mother. It pushed its dark head against her yellow-grey side and started to suck its first mouthful of milk. Its woolly coat, cleaned by its mother's tongue, was drying in the sun. It was almost entirely black.

'A Christmas lamb!' sighed Anne in wonder.

'Ah,' smiled the farmer. 'You're like me, maid. I always think there's something special about a lamb born on Christmas Day.'

And he started to sing in a surprisingly fine tenor voice,

'See amid the winter's snow ...'

They all joined in with him.

'Born for us on earth below.
See the Lamb of God appears,
Promised from eternal years.'

The fat young man sang a rich bass. When the last ringing notes of

'Christ is born in Bethlehem'

had died away, the older farmer picked the newborn

lamb up and tucked him under his arm.

'Come on, my little man. You've had a cold coming, seemingly. But we've got a warm barn waiting for you, and there'll be a bite of sweet hay for your mother. She's done a fine job for us this morning.'

He carried the lamb lovingly to the trailer. His son man-handled the heavy ewe up after it. She went willingly into the trailer after her son and nuzzled his familiar-smelling wool.

'Are you going to take him down to the farm now, and feed him with a bottle?' Anne asked.

'Not him! His own mother's milk will be better for him than an old bottle. He'll do fine enough now, thanks to you. But he'll be glad for us to give him some shelter, a day like this.'

'Is it all right if we come down with you? I'd like to use your phone, if I may. Our travel plans went a bit haywire last night. We got stuck in the drifts on the other side of the hill. We've had to sleep in the car,' Dad explained.

'Go on! Is that a fact? Well, I never! Soon as I saw you, I said to Phil here I wondered what you were doing out so early, Christmas morning. But that ewe'll be more than glad you were. She was pretty near her time when you found her. So you've been stuck in your car all last night, have you? I reckon you must have been caught out by the weather forecast, same as we were. If I'd have thought it was going to snow like that, we'd have rounded up our ewes before dark. I'd have had them down snug in the home field, not left up here on the hills in a blizzard.'

His big son Philip had grinned at them while his father talked, but hadn't said a word himself since the carol finished. Now he was in the driving-seat, turning the tractor round.

'All ready, then? Let's get this lot back home. I reckon Mum'll have the frying-pan on the go by now. And then I shall have to see if we can dig your car out.'

He jumped down from the cab again. Suddenly Anne felt herself being lifted off the ground. The young farmer swung her up into the trailer, with all the wet woolly sheep and the little black lamb. They swayed and jolted their way down the steep field, with Ian and Dad and the older farmer walking behind. Anne crinkled her nose at the smell of diesel and damp wool and the steamy breath of the sheep.

They had almost reached the bottom, and now a wonderful new smell of bacon and eggs was drifting across the yard.

'Lead me to it!' sighed Ian. 'I didn't know hot food could smell that good!'

'Mother! Put another round of rashers on. We've

got visitors!' the farmer called out, winking at them.

The farmhouse kitchen door was opening. A woman almost as tall and plump as her son Philip appeared. Her face was just broadening into a surprised but welcoming smile when Anne gasped,

'Dad! We forgot to signal to tell Mum and Sam where we were going!'

8

Together Again

Mum and Sam were left alone in the car. They watched the brightly dressed figures of Anne and Ian and Dad trudge slowly up the huge white field. Before they reached the top they had become small black specks. Then, quite suddenly, the snow seemed to flash in Sam's face like a giant mirror as it caught the newly-risen sun.

'Ow!' gasped Sam. 'It's so bright it's hurting my eyes.'

'Isn't it wonderful?' said Mum. 'It's as good as Switzerland. Well, almost! Look, every twig on every bush is covered in snow, and it's all shining.'

'It prettier than the picture on your calendar in the kitchen,' Sam said, snuggling up to Mum.

She squinted up at the sparkling snowfield against the deep-blue sky.

'They've gone!' she said.

'Who?'

'Ian and Anne and Dad, stupid.'

Mum peered up the hill through the dazzling ice on the windscreen.

'I should have brought my sun-glasses . . . You're right, though. There's not a hair of them to be seen. Don't say they've dashed off somewhere without telling us. The rotters.'

The field looked enormously big and white and empty now. In spite of the sunshine, it was very cold in the car. Sam couldn't help herself. She started to cry a little.

'I feel a bit weepy myself,' confessed Mum, cuddling her. 'I hope they won't be gone for too long. I'm really glad Spud stayed to look after us, aren't you?'

'Mmm,' agreed Sam, hugging her bear, and sniffing a bit.

Mum got into her sleeping bag again and took Sam and Spud with her, on her knee. It was a tight fit, but they helped to keep each other warm.

'It's a good job it's you two,' she laughed. 'I don't think Ian or Anne would have managed it.'

'Where did they go?'

'Search me. My eyes were so full of sunshine I didn't notice. They must have seen something. They wouldn't just have gone off and left us.'

'Pigs. They could have waved to tell us.'

'They'll be back soon.'

But they weren't.

Mum and Sam played *'One finger, one thumb, one arm, one leg, keep moving.'* It is very difficult to stand up and turn round when two of you are sitting in a car inside the same sleeping bag. They fell about and laughed a lot, but they felt warmer and happier afterwards.

The sun climbed higher in the sky. It shone down dazzlingly on the snowdrifts all around them. Sam sucked her thumb and nudged her head against Mum.

She murmured, 'Tell me a story.'

'What sort of story?'

'A Christmas story, of course.'

'Well. Once upon a time, there were shepherds up on the hills, looking after their sheep on a cold winter's night, when ...'

There was something happening at the top of the road. They saw a flurry of white, like a snowstorm, against the clear blue sky. Something dark broke into sight, a small, square tower. Sam tried to jump off Mum's knee, but she had forgotten about the sleeping bag.

'What is it? What's happening?'

'I think it's a snow-plough,' said Mum, starting to get excited too. 'No it's not. It's a tractor.'

In front was a huge yellow scoop. It dug into the

snow and tossed it aside into the hedges. There were figures tramping down the hill behind it, following its wheelmarks.

'It's them!' cried Mum. 'I can see Dad and Anne. They're bringing help.'

'Wave to them, Spud!' shouted Sam, grabbing his furry arm. 'They're coming to rescue us!'

The tractor was digging a path right down to the car. Ian was riding in the cab with the big farmer's son. Soon everybody was hugging somebody else and jumping up and down, partly with excitement and partly because their feet were cold.

'This is Mr Pring,' said Dad. 'A good shepherd, if ever there was one.'

'And Philip let me work the shovel!' Ian shouted from the cab.

'Merry Christmas to both of you,' said Mr Pring, with a cheerful smile for Mum and Sam.

'Three of us,' corrected Sam, holding up the bear. 'You mustn't forget Spud.'

'Ah. And the compliments of the season to you too, Mr Spud,' said the farmer, shaking Spud by the paw. 'Does he eat bacon and eggs?'

'I do!' sighed Mum. 'Where? Lead me to it.'

'Good job you tied that red flag on your car,' grinned big Philip, who had found his voice at last. 'From up top you looked just like another snowdrift.

I could have ploughed right into you before I noticed you, else. Proper job, that is.'

'It's mine.'

Sam took back her red shirt from him proudly.

They tied a tow-rope to the car. Dad got behind the steering-wheel while the tractor took the strain. Everyone agreed that this time it was Sam's turn to ride with Philip in the tractor-cab. She sat high up over everybody else's heads, looking out over the top of the hedges at the fairytale countryside.

The others walked beside the tractor. They were watching more anxiously as the big wheels ground up the slippery surface of the hill. There was a burst of cheering when it got to the top.

A second breakfast was ready at the farmhouse. Spud decided he didn't feel like bacon and eggs, but he did dip a paw into Sam's bread and honey, and was very sticky for the rest of the day.

It was the middle of the morning before they reached Granny and Grandad's house. The church bells were ringing out for joy down the street of grey stone cottages. Granny flung the door open, even before they had time to knock.

'Well, here you are at last, bless you! Like a Polar expedition come back to base camp. Come in out of the snow and get yourselves warm. We were beginning to wonder what on earth had happened

to you, when we didn't hear anything from you all night. And then the phone rang to say you were just up the hill. So I popped the turkey in the oven and put the Christmas pudding on to boil, and here you are. Merry Christmas, love!'

Granny hugged Sam. She wasn't a bit like the grannies in most of Sam's picture books. She was a tall, lively woman, with jet-black hair. She loved to get her boots on and go walking over Dartmoor. She didn't look old enough to be Mum's mother. Grandad was greyer than she was, but his eyes still twinkled behind his spectacles.

'So the wandering sheep have returned to the fold, have they? Sounds to me as if you've had quite a night of it. Come in and sit by the fire. I've got the kettle on.'

'Were you very worried about us?' asked Mum, kissing him.

Granny made a face. 'He was! When it came on to snow so hard, I said you'd probably stop somewhere for the night. It's true we did expect you to phone. But then we heard on the radio the blizzard had brought some telephone wires down. I kept telling your father, they're sensible people. They're sure to be all right.'

'Go on. That's her story.' Grandad winked at the children. 'She was just going to ring the police to report you missing when your Dad phoned us.'

'We weren't as sensible as we should have been,' Dad confessed.

'Well, I must say, we did send up a little prayer for you all, when we went to church for the midnight service,' Granny admitted. 'Grandad and I had a hard enough job struggling that far, even though we do live so close. But we've never missed Christmas night yet.'

'We spent the whole night in the car up on the hill,' Ian told them. '*And* we rescued a sheep.'

'And we saw a lamb being born on Christmas morning!' Anne cried out.

'And Dad used my red shirt for a flag, so Spud and me wouldn't be scooped up by the tractor!' Sam shouted.

'My! It sounds as though you *have* had an adventure,' smiled Grandad. 'Still, you're here with us now, and all's well.'

As they started to troop into the living-room, Sam caught sight of something in front of the Christmas tree.

'You've got one too! A stable and a manger and a baby lamb. It's just like ours at home.'

She picked up the tiny carved lamb and stroked it. Ian and Anne looked at each other, remembering a warm and living lamb, born in the snow.

'Well, that's what this is all about it, isn't it,' chuckled Grandad. 'More important than all the presents and the turkey and the parties, that Christmas baby there.'

Anne caught Granny's sleeve as the others crowded towards the fire. 'Were you and Grandad really praying for us in church at midnight?' she asked. 'And did they ring the church bells like they're doing now?'

'Of course they did! To welcome the Christ-child to earth.'

'Then that's what I heard ringing when we were in the car. I did, didn't I, Mum?'

'Well, I'm not sure. We were more than two miles away from Granny's church. I don't see how it could have been that.'

'But I did hear music from somewhere. I told you.'

'I expect it was angels,' said Sam.

Granny caught the girls' eyes and gave both of them a secret smile. 'Why not, love? On Christmas night, something very special indeed was happening.'

Sam had been hiding the last of the green-and-red-wrapped parcels behind her back. She brought them out and handed one to Granny and the other to Grandad. She stood on tiptoe to kiss Granny.

'Happy Christmas from Spud and me!'

Granny hugged her.

'And a wonderful Christmas it is too, now *all* the lambs are here.'

More stories from Lion Publishing

THE BOY WHO WOULDN'T

Veronica Heley

'I'll be so bad to the new people that they'll sell their house back to the Biker. Then everything will be all right again,' thought Joe.

It is the worst day of Joe's life. His only friend has moved away and there are new people living next door. But not for long—if Joe has anything to do with it.

ISBN 0 7459 1967 7

NO PROBLEM, DAVY

Peggy Burns

'Davy remembered what his dad had said. He must not untie the lead from the post. But what difference was it going to make? He would just let Patch have a little run. Dogs needed to run around, didn't they? He reached out and unclipped the lead. No problem . . .
Before Davy could stop him, Patch dashed away down the road. Davy stared after him in horror.'

Nine thoughtful and reassuring stories about the everyday adventures of six-year-old Davy and his family.

ISBN 0 7459 2076 4

THE BROWN-EARS STORIES

Stephen Lawhead

Brown-Ears, the lop-eared, happy-go-lucky, fuzzy cloth rabbit was more than just forgetful. He was positively careless—especially when it came to getting lost.

Two delightful adventures of a lost-and-found rabbit that will bering a smile to anyone who has lost a favourite friend.

BROWN-EARS
ISBN 0 7459 1548 5

BROWN-EARS AT SEA
ISBN 0 7459 1926 X

UNDER THE GOLDEN THRONE

Ralph Batten

'Under the golden throne, in the palace of the High King,
lay Shamar, the one and only dog of Patria. Slowly he
yawned and opened a big, brown eye...'

In the seven tales of Shamar the dog, we meet a wealth of
comic characters, including the self-important Prime Min-
ister of Patria, the fussy Chancellor of the Exchequer and the
dignified Derel the Wise. And, of course, the delightfully
stupid Seven Knights of the Realm.

Each story tells of an adventure of Shamar the dog and
his beloved master, the High King of Patria. And at the end
of each story, Shamar settles down under the golden throne
and sleeps. And as he sleeps, he dreams a dream...

ISBN 0 85648 780 5

IN THE KINGDOM OF THE CARPET DRAGON

Ralph Batten

'You have been given a royal gift and a task which you must perform. It is your adventure ... You alone must decide when to use this stone,' said the Emperor.

Princess Anah was surprised when her royal birthday gift turned out to be nothing more than a stone on a golden chain. But this ordinary-looking stone could have great power in the Kingdom of the Carpet Dragon. It was up to the Princess to discover what that power was, and when and how to use it ...

Accompanied by her lovable, loyal and remarkably clumsy pet dragon, Doxa, the Princess sets out on her quest—with some surprising results.

ISBN 0 7459 1533 7

THE HAFFERTEE STORIES

Janet and John Perkins

Haffertee is a soft-toy hamster. Ma Diamond made him for her little girl, Yolanda (usually known as Diamond Yo), when her real pet hamster died.

These books tell the adventures of the inquisitive, amusing and lovable Haffertee Hamster—at home, at school and in the world outside.

There are six Haffertee books in the series. Illustrated with line drawings, each contains ten short stories, ideal for bedtime reading or reading aloud.

A selection of top titles for young readers from LION PUBLISHING

THE BOY WHO WOULDN'T Veronica Heley	£2.25☐
NO PROBLEM, DAVY Peggy Burns	£2.50☐
UNDER THE GOLDEN THRONE Ralph Batten	£1.99☐
IN THE KINGDOM OF THE CARPET DRAGON Ralph Batten	£1.99☐
BROWN-EARS Stephen Lawhead	£1.75☐
BROWN-EARS AT SEA Stephen Lawhead	£2.25☐
HAFFERTEE HAMSTER Janet and John Perkins	£2.25☐
HAFFERTEE'S NEW HOUSE Janet and John Perkins	£2.25☐
HAFFERTEE GOES EXPLORING Janet and John Perkins	£2.25☐
HAFFERTEE'S FIRST CHRISTMAS Janet and John Perkins	£2.25☐
HAFFERTEE GOES TO SCHOOL Janet and John Perkins	£2.25☐
HAFFERTEE'S FIRST EASTER Janet and John Perkins	£2.25☐
THE DAY THE FAIR CAME	£1.75☐

All Lion paperbacks are available from your local bookshop or newsagent, or can be ordered direct from the address below. Just tick the titles you want and fill in the form.

Name (Block letters)

Address

Write to Lion Publishing, Cash Sales Department, PO Box 11, Falmouth, Cornwall TR10 9EN, England.

Please enclose a cheque or postal order to the value of the cover price plus:

UK: 80p for the first book, 20p for each additional book ordered to a maximum charge of £2.00.

OVERSEAS INCLUDING EIRE: £1.50 for the first book, £1.00 for the second book and 30p for each additional book.

BFPO: 80p for the first book, 20p for each additional book.

Lion Publishing reserves the right to show on covers and charge new retail prices which may differ from those previously advertised in the text or elsewhere, and to increase postal rates in accordance with the Post Office.